Bordaria
Difendere con Coraggio

Scholastic Canada Ltd.
604 King Street West, Toronto, Ontario M5V 1E1, Canada

Scholastic Inc.
557 Broadway, New York, NY 10012, USA

Scholastic Australia Pty Limited
PO Box 579, Gosford, NSW 2250, Australia

Scholastic New Zealand Limited
Private Bag 94407, Botany, Manukau 2163, New Zealand

Scholastic Children's Books
Euston House, 24 Eversholt Street, London NW1 1DB, UK

PÖP & F!ZZ

Text, design and illustration copyright © Lemonfizz Media, 2010.
Cover illustration by Melanie Matthews
Internal illustrations by Lionel Portier, Melanie Matthews and James Hart.
First published by Pop & Fizz and Scholastic Australia in 2010.
Pop & Fizz is a partnership between Paddlepop Press and Lemonfizz Media.
www.paddlepoppress.com
This edition published under licence from Scholastic Australia Pty Limited
on behalf of Lemonfizz Media.

First published by Scholastic Australia in 2010.
This edition published by Scholastic Canada Ltd., 2011.

Library and Archives Canada Cataloguing in Publication

Park, Mac

Infernix / Mac Park ; illustrations by Melanie Matthews, Lionel Portier and James Hart.

(Boy vs beast. Battle of the worlds)

ISBN 978-1-4431-0749-5

I. Matthews, Melanie, 1986- II. Portier, Lionel
III. Hart, James, 1981- IV. Title. V. Series: Park, Mac.
Boy vs beast. Battle of the worlds.

PZ7.P2213In 2011   j823'.92   C2010-907356-8

BOY vs BEAST

BEAST

BATTLE OF THE WORLDS

INFERNIX

Mac Park

POP & F!ZZ
◼ SCHOLASTIC

Prologue

Once, mega-beast and man shared one world. But it did not last. The beasts wanted to rule the world. They started battles against man. After many bad battles between beast and man, the world was split in two. Man was given Earth. Mega-beasts were given Beastium.

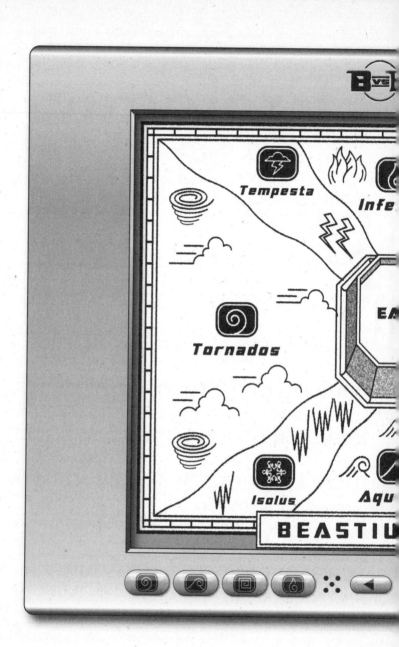

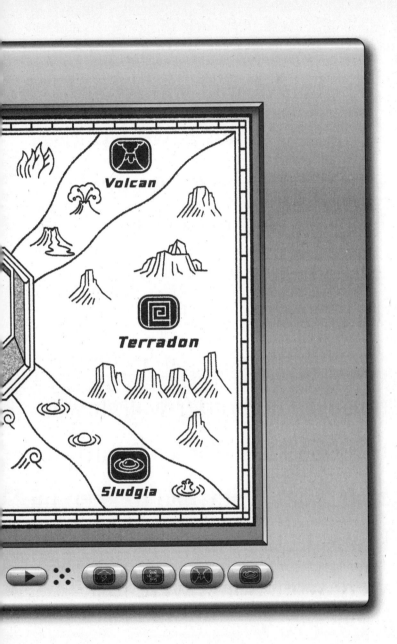

Volcan

Terradon

Sludgia

A border-wall was created. It closed the two worlds off. Man was safe. But not for long . . . Beastium was not enough for the mega-beasts. They wanted Earth.

The beasts began to battle through the border-wall. It was the job of the Border Guards to stop them. They had to keep the beasts in Beastium. Some battles were won. Some were lost.

Battles won by the beasts gave them more power. The beasts earned new battle attacks. Battles won by the Border Guards earned them upgrades. Their battle gear could do more.

Five boys now guard the border-wall. They are the Bordaria Border Guards. They are in training to become Border Masters like their dads.

The Bordaria Master Command

The Border Guards' dads and granddads are the Bordaria Master Command. The BMC helps the Border Guards during battle.

The Border Guards must learn. The safety of Earth depends on them.

The BMC rewards good Border Guard battling. Upgrades can be earned for sending beasts back into their lands. New battle gear can also be given to Border Guards who battle well.

If they do not battle well, the Border Guards will lose upgrades and points. Then they will not be given new and better gear.

Kai Masters is a Border Guard in training. His work is top secret. He must protect Earth. The BMC watches Kai closely. Kai must not fail.

Let the battles commence!

Chapter 1

It was Sunday. It was a very hot day. Kai Masters was at the waterslide park. There were lots of kids there.

Kai was in one of the big pools. He was floating around on his back. Kai felt nice and cool.

Kai Masters was twelve years old. He was also a Border Guard. Border Guards kept Earth safe from beasts.

The beasts lived in Beastium. But they wanted Earth. Sometimes the beasts tried to crash through the border-wall. The wall was between the beasts' world and Earth. Kai's job was to stop them from getting through.

Kai had to keep the beasts in their own lands. Sometimes he had to battle them to do that. But he didn't go into battle alone. Kai had the help of his dogbot, BC3. Kai called him BC for short. BC knew how to battle well. He had legs that could move at top speeds.

BC's fast legs were handy in battles. They also made him an ace soccer player. BC was Kai's buddy. Kai thought BC was great to play soccer with.

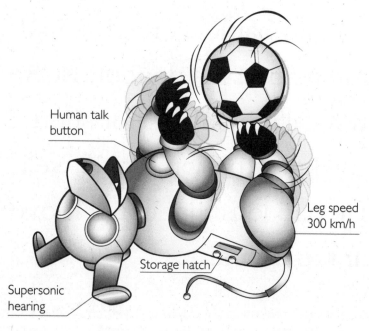

Human talk button

Leg speed 300 km/h

Storage hatch

Supersonic hearing

BC was a gift from the Border Masters. They made up the Master Command, the BMC. The BMC helped Border Guards learn to battle well.

The BMC used an orbix to talk with their guards. It was a small round computer. Every border guard had one. Kai's orb had a space inside it.

Kai often kept things in the orb's space. Things Kai might need in battle. Or things that he wanted to look at later.

THE ORBIX

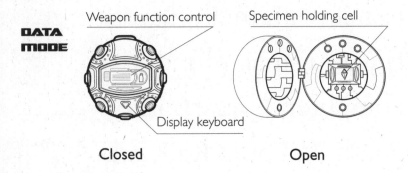

DATA MODE

Weapon function control

Specimen holding cell

Display keyboard

Closed

Open

Kai swam around in the pool. *Maybe I'll go on the waterslide,* he thought. Just then a man called out, "Quick, the garbage can is on fire!" People came running to see.

Kai went to the side of the pool. He saw the man throw lots of water into the can. But the fire kept going.

That's strange, thought Kai. *It's just a small fire. Why didn't the water put it out?*

The pool guard ran to the can. He had a foam-blaster that puts out fires. The guard filled the can with foam. The fire went out.

Everyone went back to the pools. Everyone but Kai. He looked in the can. It was filled with ash. *Just black stuff left over from the fire,* thought Kai. *But why did it need fire-foam? I hope a beast hasn't done this.*

Kai opened his orb. He used it to scoop up some ash. Then he closed the orb. *I'd better test this in my lab,* thought Kai.

Chapter 2

Kai lived in the lighthouse on the hill. It had some great things in it. There was a secret elevator. It went from the bottom to the top of the lighthouse. Only Kai and BC could use it. There was also a game room. It had a bowling alley in it.

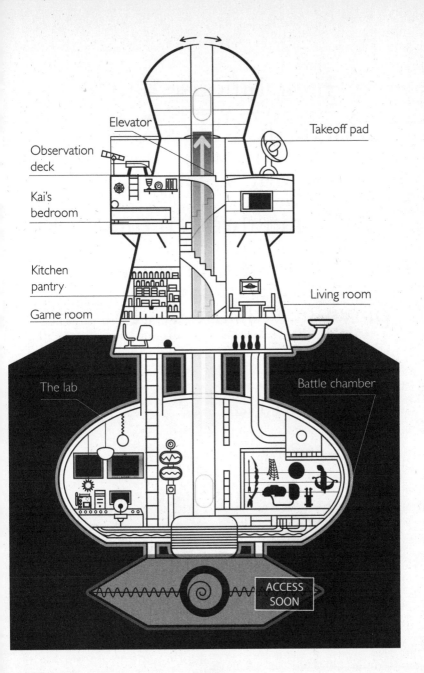

Elevator

Takeoff pad

Observation deck

Kai's bedroom

Kitchen pantry

Living room

Game room

The lab

Battle chamber

ACCESS SOON

The lighthouse had a hidden lab. Kai used it to learn about beasts.

Kai ran through the back door. He could hear BC playing with the soccer ball. "Stop playing and look at this, BC," said Kai.

BC looked at the ash. His tail started to wag. "Trouble," said BC. BC's tail always wagged when there was trouble.

"Yes," said Kai. "We need to test it. Let's go to the lab."

The lab's ladder was behind the kitchen pantry wall. Kai went into the pantry. He pushed the button under the bottom shelf.

The back wall of the pantry began to move. Kai and BC went down the ladder into the lab.

"I should not touch this ash," said Kai. "It needs to stay in the orb. I'm going to use the orb mini lab." Kai put the orb into the mini lab. The mini lab had a remote control. Kai hit a button. Lights filled the mini lab.

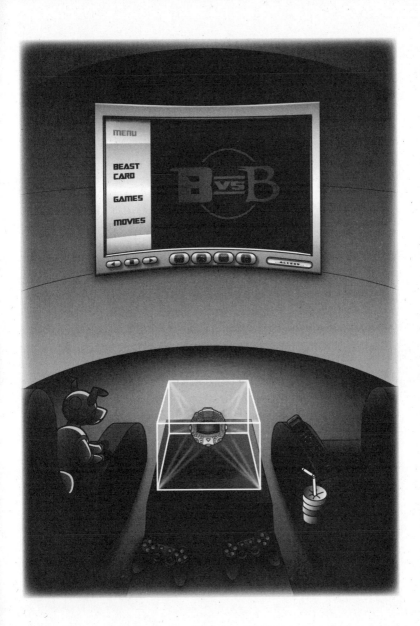

Words flashed onto the remote control's screen.

A map came up on the wall screen. Kai and BC both looked at it.

"Two border-lands and the fire land," said Kai. "That's a bit strange.

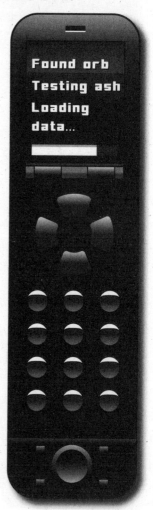

On the remote control's screen:

Found orb
Testing ash
Loading data...

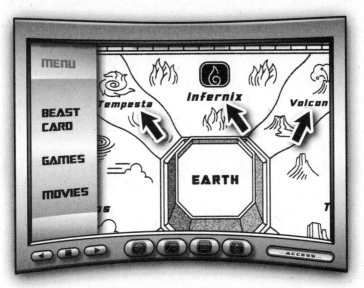

It can't be three places."

Kai picked up the remote.

He spoke into the phone.

Kai said, "The fire was put out with foam. Water didn't work."

The screen went black. Then just the fire land came up. Kai spoke into the phone again. "Show beast," said Kai. A card popped up.

"It's only a little beast," said Kai. He tried to call up the next beast card. He wanted to see if the beast had changed. Nothing happened. "This will be an easy battle," said Kai. "Come on, BC. We need to get our battle gear."

Chapter 3

Kai took out his Border Guard Card. It let him into the battle chamber. He put his card into the computer.

Name........... **Kai Masters**
Rank........... **Border Guard**
Guard Post... **Lighthouse**
Age............. **12**
Home Element... **Fire**

41352461

Bordaria
Difendere con Coraggio

CLUNK BANG!
Whiiiiir!
BANG!

Four bricks in the wall behind him began to move.

The bricks left a space. Kai and BC climbed through it. The battle chamber had three walls. Two walls had battle gear on them.

The third wall had a screen over it. Kai could not see through it. "We still can't see what's on wall three," said Kai. "What can we take?"

"That one on the middle wall?" asked BC.

"Could be good," said Kai. He went to take it. They heard a noise.

CLUNK! GRRRR
CLUNK!

Then a computer voice said,

"Soon."

"The BMC still has wall two locked, BC," said Kai. "But soon it won't be. Maybe if I win this battle. Let's look at wall one."

Kai went to the first wall. "This looks good, BC," he said. "It shoots foam. Foam put the fire out in the can."

FOAM-BLASTER

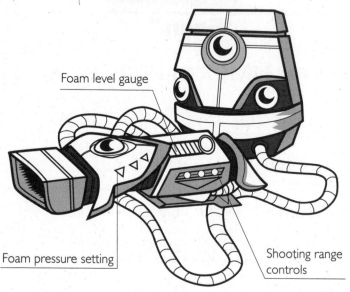

Foam level gauge

Foam pressure setting

Shooting range controls

"This can shoot a long way," said Kai. "I'm taking it. We can have one more thing from this room."

Kai thought about the beast on the card. "I bet that beast will throw fire at us," said Kai. "We need to stop the fire from getting us. What about this?"

DEFENCE SHIELD

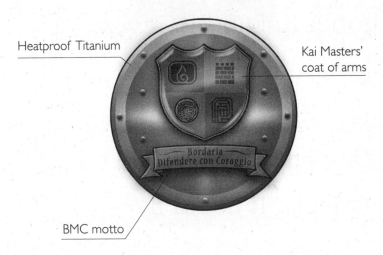

Heatproof Titanium

Kai Masters' coat of arms

Bordaria
Difendere con Coraggio

BMC motto

"This can block the hottest fire. It will be good," said Kai. "Come on, let's get out of here." They both climbed out of the battle chamber.

The bricks moved back into place. The space was gone. Kai and BC were back in the lab again. Kai's hoverboard was on the floor. Kai picked it up. The board had jets. It could fly fast.

"We need to fly in a fire land," said Kai. He took out his orb.

Kai keyed in the code for the fire land.

17649
Infernix

"The BMC better make my clothes fireproof," said Kai.

"We'll soon see," said BC.

Kai and BC went into the elevator. Kai hit the button. The elevator went up to the top of the lighthouse. Kai stood on the takeoff pad.

"The BMC gave me a jet-pack," said BC.

"Great, you'll need it, BC," said Kai. "Let's see if we got upgrades."

Kai looked at his orb. "Yes!" he said. "Two

upgrades. One for you and one for me."

"What are they?" asked BC.

"My clothes and your body are fireproof," said Kai. "But it does wear off. Let's hope it's not too hot for too long."

Kai hit the light button on the orb. The roof of the lighthouse opened. The takeoff pad filled with light.

Kai and BC were ready to go. The light shot up into the sky. It took Kai and BC with it. To the fire land.

Chapter 4

Kai knew he was in the fire
land. It was hot. Very hot.
And there were fires
everywhere. Flames shot up
into the smoky air. Sparks of
fire flew all around them.

The land was red and dry.
It was hard to see. Kai turned
his visor to fire shield.

Just then his orb beeped.

"The shield got an upgrade," said Kai.

"What kind of upgrade?" asked BC.

"The shield can send out a force field ring," said Kai.

Suddenly, something hit Kai's visor.

Kai used his fireproof clothes to wipe it off. "That started to melt my visor," said Kai. "What was it?"

Suddenly, Kai and BC were under attack.

It was a fly attack. But not just any flies. Fire-flies.

The flies moved in a big group. And they shot red-hot blobs of goo. They went all over Kai and BC.

Kai and BC wiped off the goo. Kai put up his shield. It kept them safe from the goo. Then BC began to snap at the flies.

BC snapped one after the other. Kai laughed. It made him think of the flies at home. BC always went for them, too.

"Go, BC!" said Kai.

BC took care of all the flies. Then a bigger group of fire-flies attacked.

Splat **Splat** **Splat**

There are too many for BC, thought Kai. *But I can't waste my foam on them.*

Kai did a quick
back flip on his board.
The board's jets were
now facing the flies.
Kai turned the board's
jets to turbo. He blasted
the flies hard. All the fire-flies
fell away. "That takes care of
them," said Kai.

Chapter 5

Kai and BC hovered above the fires. Suddenly BC's heat sensors went crazy. And his tail was wagging. "It's getting hotter. Something is coming," said BC.

"Where? Out of the fire?" asked Kai. Kai looked at the fire.

He began to see the shape of something.

"Here it comes, BC," said Kai. "But it's little. This battle should be over quickly."

A small beast came out of the fire. Its tail flicked. Sparks flew up.

Then the small beast opened its mouth. It spat out a small ball of fire.

The fire-ball didn't go far at all. Kai laughed. "It's hardly worth battling," said Kai. "Come on. Let's get this over with."

The beast looked at Kai and BC. It was mad. It spat a fire-ball that sent BC flying. Another fire-ball shot out.

It almost knocked Kai
off his board.

WHACH!

Then the beast pointed its
claw and flicked it.
An even bigger fire-ball
flew from the claw. The
beast flicked its claw again
and again. Fire-balls flew
at Kai and BC. Kai and
BC could not fight back.

"Get on the board, BC," said Kai.

WHACH! WHACH! WHACH!

Kai put his shield in front of them. That was when he saw the new upgrade buttons. Kai hit the first one. Rings of white light shot out from the front of the shield.

They pushed the beast back. Its fire-balls hit the shield and fell away.

Kai pushed the beast back into a fire pit. It fell down into the fires below.

"Well, I got that little beast wrong," said Kai. "Its fire-balls had power. Let's go to the other side of the fire pit." They hovered across the fires. Then Kai's orb beeped.

Kai took out his orb. "You got an upgrade," said Kai. "A force-field bubble." Kai used his orb to turn it on. "Nice bubble, BC. I didn't get any upgrades."

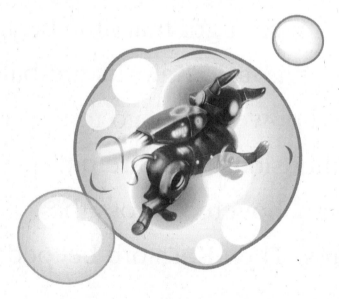

Chapter 6

BC's tail began to wag.
Kai turned to look. The little
dragon was out of the fire pit.
But it was not little any more.
It was big. The fire had made
it grow bigger and stronger.

"It has changed to a new,
bigger beast," said Kai. "I was
nuts to push it into the fire."

Kai took a photo with his orb. A card popped up.

"This one will be hard," said Kai.

Fire flew from the beast's mouth. It landed just in front of Kai.

The fire turned into a ring of fire. Kai and BC were trapped. The fire grew taller. It was now a huge fire wall.

The beast's claws were open and ready. "A claw fire-ball attack is coming. We need to get out of this ring of fire," said Kai.

Fire-balls flew from the beast's claw. Things were really heating up.

We're going to be trapped in our own fire pit!

Get on the hoverboard. We're going up.

WOOOOSSH

Kai put the hoverboard's jets on top speed. Then he flew back at the beast.

ROOOAR!

The shield is working.

My tail is wagging! Something is wrong.

The fire hit the shield and went back onto the beast. It made it grow and change. It became massive.

HSSSS!

Oh no! It's going to hit us with fire.

Put your shield down. We don't want the fire to go back to the beast again.

Good move, BC! Your force field doesn't push the fire back.

The fire hit BC's force field. But the fire didn't bounce off it.

But the fire is pushing us into another land.

Kai and BC were blasted into the border-land of fire and rock. It was filled with rivers of fire.

You got something from the BMC. I wonder what it is? Let's go back. It's time to use the foam blaster.

I hope you have enough foam for the job.

The beast was ready for them. It threw more and more fire. Kai hit the fires with foam.

It's putting out the fires but the foam is going to run out soon.

What's it doing with its tail?

The beast was very mad. It spun a tube of fire from its tail.

WOOOP.
WOOOP

It's a fire-wave attack!

And this heat is hotter than my clothes can take now!

Chapter 7

Kai and BC hovered above the border-wall. "Did you see the bubbles from the bottle, BC?" asked Kai. "They trapped those fire-balls. No air could get inside the bubble. The fire couldn't get out. Then the fire died inside the bubble."

"Those bubbles are like my force field bubble," said BC. "They can open and close around things."

"Yes," said Kai. "We need to put that beast into a bubble. Then its fire won't have air. Fire can't keep going with no air. Only dogbots can keep going with no air!"

"How do we get the beast into the bubble?" asked BC.

"I don't know," said Kai.

Just then Kai's orb flashed.

"The bottle must fit in the foam blaster," said Kai.

Kai took the lid off the

bottle. Then he took the foam tank off the blaster. He put the bubble bottle where the tank had been. Little bubbles came out of the blaster.

"I hope this works," said Kai. "The bubbles look so small."

"But the blaster has power," said BC.

"Maybe it will make big bubbles. Ready to go?" asked Kai.

"Ready," said BC.

They flew back into the fire land.

The beast saw them coming. It spun its tail once more. Another wave of fire came at Kai and BC.

"We'll have to surf the fire-wave again," said Kai.

They surfed down the fire-wave.

"Oh, no," said BC. "It's going to do a fire-ball attack, too!" Fire-balls flew out from the beast's claws. The fire-balls went down the wave.

"I've got them, BC," said Kai. Kai shot bubbles from the blaster. The bubbles trapped the fire-balls.

The fire-balls turned to ash inside the bubbles.

"Now for the big beast," said Kai. He hovered close to the beast. Kai blasted bubbles at it.

The bubbles joined in the air. They came down around the beast. They trapped the beast in one big bubble.

The wave of fire stopped.

The fire-balls stopped.

All the beast's fire went out.

The beast was finished. It lay down in the bubble. It was empty. Kai and BC had won.

Chapter 8

"The beast is trapped.
And its fire is out," said Kai.
"Now let's send it back.
Back to its home, where it
came from."

Kai turned his
hoverboard jets to turbo-
blast. He turned BC's jet
pack to turbo-blast, too.

They pointed their jets at the beast.

The jets blasted the bubble with the beast far away. Far back into the fire land. Far from the border-wall. Kai and BC couldn't see it any more.

"Home time for us, too, BC," said Kai. Just then his orb flashed. Kai took out his orb.

"I can turn off your bubble now, BC!" Kai hit the off button.

The force field bubble went away. Kai keyed in:

Dome open

White light came down from above. It shone over

Kai and BC. The light went up. It took Kai and BC with it. They were on their way home.

FLAMAXAGON

All burnt out

Battle Plays ★★★★☆

New Attacks ★☆☆☆☆

Energy ★★★★⯪

BORDER
GUARD
BATTLE
STATS

Kai Masters

What a hot ride

Battle Plays ★★★★★

Upgrades ★★★★★

Bonus Items ★★★★★

BATTLE OF THE WORLDS
Have you read them all?